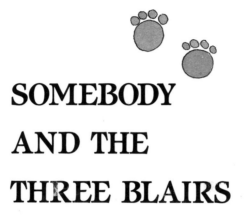

SOMEBODY
AND THE
THREE BLAIRS

Somebody and the Three Blairs

by MARILYN TOLHURST

illustrations by SIMONE ABEL

ORCHARD BOOKS · NEW YORK

Orchard Books, 95 Madison Avenue, New York, NY 10016

Manufactured in the United States of America. Printed by Barton Press, Inc. Bound by Horowitz/Rae. Book design by Mina Greenstein. The text of this book is set in 18 pt. Galliard. The illustrations are watercolor and pen-and-ink. Hardcover   10   9   8   7   6   5
Paperback   10   9   8   7   6   5   4   3   2   1

Library of Congress Cataloging-in-Publication Data
Tolhurst, Marilyn. Somebody and the three Blairs / by Marilyn Tolhurst ;
illustrated by Simone Abel.—1st American ed.   p.   cm.
Summary: In a reversal of the Goldilocks story, a bear explores the home of the three Blairs while they are out.
ISBN 0-531-05878-6 (tr.)   ISBN 0-531-08478-7 (lib. bdg.)
ISBN 0-531-07056-5 (pbk.)
[1. Bears—Fiction.]   I. Abel, Simone, ill.   II. Title.
PZ7.T5743So   1991   [E]—dc20   90-7747

For Bertie

—M. T.

To Ralph and Lilo

—S. A.

SOMEBODY
AND THE
THREE BLAIRS

One Sunday morning, in a small house on the
edge of town, Mr. Blair, Mrs. Blair, and Baby Blair
were sitting down to breakfast.

"It's such a fine morning," said Mr. Blair.
"Let's take a walk in the park."

"What a good idea," said Mrs. Blair.

"Feeda ducks," said Baby Blair.

So they took their coats and a bag of bread crumbs and set out for the park.

While they were gone, Somebody came to the door. Somebody knocked, and when no one answered, Somebody tiptoed in.

He sniffed and sniffed.
He looked at the breakfast table.
"This food is too dry," said Somebody.

"This food is too noisy,"
said Somebody.

"But this food is just right."

He looked for somewhere to sit down.

"This seat is too hard,"
said Somebody.

"This seat is too wobbly,"
said Somebody.

"But this seat is just right."

He looked for something to play with.

"This game is too noisy,"
said Somebody.

"This game is too cold,"
said Somebody.

"But this game is just right."

He looked for something to drink.

"This rain is too hot,"
said Somebody.

"This pond is too small,"
said Somebody.

"But this stream is just right."

He looked for somewhere to sleep.

"This bed is too big,"
said Somebody.

"This bed is too small,"
said Somebody.

"But this bed is just right."

When Mr. and Mrs. Blair and Baby Blair came
back from the park, they saw the breakfast table.

"Somebody's been eating
my Crunchies," said Mr. Blair.

"Somebody's been eating
my Crispies," said Mrs. Blair.

"All gone!" said Baby Blair.

They looked around the room.

"Somebody's been sitting on my chair," said Mr. Blair.

"Somebody's been sitting on *my* chair," said Mrs. Blair.

"Busted!" said Baby Blair.

They went into the kitchen.

"Somebody's been emptying the cupboard," said Mr. Blair.

"Somebody's been raiding the fridge," said Mrs. Blair.

"Naughty!" said Baby Blair.

They went upstairs.

"Flood!" shouted Mr. Blair.
"Help!" shouted Mrs. Blair.
"Lotta water!" shouted Baby Blair.

They looked in the bedrooms.

"It's a burglar,"
said Mr. Blair.

"It's a monster,"
said Mrs. Blair.

"Issa big teddy bear,"
said Baby Blair.

"It's escaped from the zoo," said Mr. Blair.

"It's escaped from the circus," said Mrs. Blair.

"Iss escaped downa drainpipe," said Baby Blair.

"Somebody phone the police!" said Mr. Blair.

"Somebody call the fire department!" said Mrs. Blair.

"Somebody gone home," said Baby Blair.

"Bye-bye. Come again and play tomorrow."